# Bad Jack Fox

Written by Russell Punter

Illustrated by Colin Jack

# How this book works

The story of **Bad Jack Fox** has been written for you to read with your child. You take turns to read:

**You read these words.**

Dan opens up his diamond store. He's watched by Bad Jack Fox. "I wonder what Dan's carrying?"

"I will rob him of his box."

4

5

**Your child reads these words.**

You don't have to finish the story in one session. If your child is getting tired, put a marker in the page and come back to it later.

You can find out more about helping your child with this book, and with reading in general, on pages 30-31.

# Bad Jack Fox

Turn the page to start the story.

Dan opens up his diamond store.
He's watched by Bad Jack Fox.
"I wonder what Dan's carrying?"

"I will rob him
of his box."

Jack grabs the box and runs away.
"Hey, wait, stop thief!" cries Dan.

But Dan is not
as quick as Jack.

Zip! He is off
in his van.

Dan spots a friend in his taxi cab.
"Mick's sure to help, I know."
Dan has a plan.
   "Just follow that van!"

The cab goes fast, but then it stops.
"Tank's empty – just my luck!"

But I will go
and get a can.

While Mick is filling up the tank,
Dan's thinking of Bad Jack.
"My box is miles away by now."

I will not get it back.

"Don't worry," says Mick,
as they zoom away.
"I'll soon return your box."

17

Now who's that in the road ahead?
Looks like he needs a tow.

It is Jack Fox
and his red van.

Bad luck!
It will not go.

19

The van lets out a cloud of smoke.
Mick peers inside. "What's this?
You need to let your engine cool."

Dan quickly grabs his precious box.
He's glad to get it back.
"A bath toy for my son, you see."

# Puzzle 1

Look at the pictures, then read the
sentences and answer True or False.

1.

## Jack Fox has a box.

2.

## Dan cannot get a cab.

3.

Dan is sad.

4.

Jack Fox is fed up!

# Puzzle 2

There is one wrong word in the sentences below each picture. What should they say?

1.

Dan is not as quack as Jack.

2.

Zip! He is off in his can.

3.

"I will mix Jack Fox."

4.

"Bad duck! It will not go."

# Puzzle 3

Choose the right words for each picture.

# Answers to puzzles

**Puzzle 1**

1. False
2. False
3. True
4. True

**Puzzle 2**

1. Dan is not as ~~queck~~ as Jack.
   Dan is not as quick as Jack.
2. Zip! He is off in his ~~ean~~.
   Zip! He is off in his van.
3. I will ~~mix~~ Jack Fox.
   I will fix Jack Fox.
4. Bad ~~duck!~~ It will not go.
   Bad luck! It will not go.

**Puzzle 3**

1. C   Quick, Mick!
2. B   Fizz! Hiss!
3. A   Quack quack!

# Guidance notes

**Usborne Very First Reading** is a series of books, specially developed for children who are learning to read. In the early books in the series, you and your child take turns to read, and your child steadily builds the knowledge and confidence to read alone.

The words for your child to read in **Bad Jack Fox** introduce these eight letters or letter-combinations:

| | | | | | | | |
|---|---|---|---|---|---|---|---|
| **j** | **qu** | **v** | **w** | **x** | **y** | **z** | **zz** |

It's important for your child to recognize these combinations and their sounds, not just read the letters individually. Be aware that this represents a more challenging stage in their reading, too. Later books in the series gradually introduce more letter-combinations and spelling patterns, while reinforcing the ones your child already knows.

You'll find lots more information about the structure of the series, advice on helping your child with reading, extra practice activities and games on the Very First Reading website,* **www.usborne.com/veryfirstreading**

*US readers go to **www.veryfirstreading.com**

# Some questions and answers

- **Why do I need to read with my child?**
  Sharing stories and taking turns makes reading an enjoyable and fun activity for children. It also helps them to develop confidence and reading stamina, and to take part in an exciting story using very few words.

- **When is a good time to read?**
  Choose a time when you are both relaxed, but not too tired, and there are no distractions. Only read for as long as your child wants to – you can always try again another day.

- **What if my child gets stuck?**
  Don't simply read the problem word yourself, but prompt your child and try to find the right answer together. Similarly, if your child makes a mistake, go back and look at the word together. Don't forget to give plenty of praise and encouragement.

- **We've finished, now what do we do?**
  It's a good idea to read the story several times to give your child more practice and confidence. Then you can try reading **Dog Diary** at the same level or, when your child is ready, go on to Book 5 in the series.

Edited by Jenny Tyler, Lesley Sims
and Mairi MacKinnon

First published in 2011 by Usborne Publishing Ltd., Usborne House,
83-85 Saffron Hill, London EC1N 8RT, England. www.usborne.com
Copyright © 2011 Usborne Publishing Ltd.

# USBORNE VERY FIRST READING

There are twenty-four titles in the **Usborne Very First Reading** series, which has been specially developed to help children learn to read.

To find out more about the structure of the series, go to **www.usborne.com/veryfirstreading**

1

1

2

2

3

3

4

4

5

5